First published in 1995 by Ultimate Editions

© 1995 Anness Publishing Limited

Ultimate Editions is an imprint of
Anness Publishing Limited
Boundary Row Studios
1 Boundary Row
London SE1 8HP

ISBN 1 86035 016 X

Editorial Director Joanna Lorenz
Editorial Consultant Jackie Fortey
Project Editor Belinda Wilkinson

Printed and bound in China

A Storyteller Book

Aladdin

Retold by Lesley Young

Illustrated by Govinder Nazran

ULTIMATE
EDITIONS

A long time ago, in China, there lived a boy called Aladdin. His father had died and he and his mother were very poor. They lived in a very small house near the edge of the town, and his mother made a little money by washing and ironing huge piles of laundry.

"Where are you, Aladdin? Come and help me wring out these towels," shouted his mother, looking out the kitchen door. But Aladdin was off wandering in the countryside, as usual. He loved to walk in the fields and dream up all sorts of new plans for becoming rich.

Suddenly a stranger appeared and began patting Aladdin on the back. He could not recall having seen the man before, which wasn't surprising because he was really a wicked magician in disguise.

"Aladdin, don't you recognize your old Uncle Ebenezer?"

"I've just come home from my travels abroad and I'm really glad I've bumped into you, because I need your help."

He took Aladdin's arm and marched him through the fields until they came to a grassy bank with a stone slab in its side.

"There's a cave behind here," went on the magician. "I would love to climb inside myself, but I'm afraid I'm too fat. But you could slip in like an eel. There's an old oil lamp in there I want. It looks ordinary, but I'm rather attached to it."

Then the magician warned, "But beware, you must not touch anything else you see in the cave!"

Aladdin was curious to see what the cave looked like. He was always hoping an adventure would turn up. Perhaps this was one. So he held his breath and wriggled through the narrow opening and down a few rough stone steps into a large cave.

A dim light shone down from the opening above, and it took Aladdin's eyes some time to get used to the gloom. But when they did, they grew wider and wider. On all sides were piles of gold, silver and jewels. In the corner was a gold statue with a diamond necklace and a silver crown. In its hand was a dull old oil lamp, looking out of place among the sparkling riches.

Despite the magician's warning, Aladdin could not resist stuffing necklaces and gold coins into his pockets.

'Mother will never have to wash even a hankie again,' he smiled to himself.

"Have you found the lamp?" boomed a loud voice.

Aladdin had forgotten all about the magician.

"I'm coming," he called back, trying to slip more gold coins into his shoes.

"Hurry up!" shouted the magician. "I'm warning you, I won't wait much longer."

Aladdin fetched the old oil lamp and shuffled over to the stairs. But he was so weighted down with gold and jewels that he couldn't wriggle back out.

"I can't leave all this behind," he wailed. "Uncle, I don't know what to do."

"I'll tell you what you can do," screamed the magician, who was tired of waiting, "you can stay there forever!"

There was a thud and everything went black. Aladdin was trapped inside.

'What good are all these riches if I never get out of this dark cave?' he thought.

He began to feel his way round the cave. He felt the foot of the statue, and beside it the old oil lamp which he had dropped when the slab slammed shut. 'I wonder why uncle wanted this old thing, when he could have had all these jewels,' he said to himself, as he sat down clutching the lamp.

It was nearly dinner time, and when Aladdin thought of his mother putting a bowl of tasty rice and fish on the table, a tear fell on the lamp. Without thinking, he rubbed it away with his sleeve.

FLASH!

There was a huge bang and the cave was lit up by bright lights, like fireworks, making the gold and jewels dazzle. Then a wisp of white smoke curled out of the spout of the oil lamp. Aladdin pressed himself against the cave wall, as first a face and then an enormous body appeared in the air above him.

"At last! I thought I was stuck in there for another hundred years!" boomed a loud voice.

Then the huge man with polished brown skin swung his long pigtail around as he noticed Aladdin. At once he bowed to him, golden hoops glittering in his ears: "The Genie of the lamp, Master, at your service. I have been waiting for a hundred years for someone to rub the lamp and let me out."

"Now, what is your wish?"

'This is probably all a dream,' thought Aladdin.

"I would like to go home, to my mother, please." he said.

There was another flash, and instantly Aladdin found himself in his mother's kitchen, still clutching the lamp.

Aladdin's mother was about to scold him for being late, but when he pulled the gold and diamonds out of his pockets, she fell back on a pile of newly-ironed sheets and gasped.

"But that's not the best thing," said Aladdin, "Our troubles are over – we can have whatever we want, thanks to the Genie of the lamp." His mother didn't believe him, so he rubbed the lamp and the Genie appeared.

"Send all the washing back, and fetch us a banquet with roast duck," commanded Aladdin.

Then a table set with mouth-watering dishes arrived in front of them and his mother had to believe him.

"When we've had enough to eat," said Aladdin, "we'll ask the Genie to build us a fine house to live in."

Soon they were happily settled in their new large white villa.

Not long afterwards, Aladdin was walking through the market when the crowd scattered to let a gold carriage through.

Looking inside as the carriage flew past, Aladdin saw a girl with long black hair and eyes like violets. She was even more beautiful than all his new treasures.

"Who is she?" he asked a stall holder.

"That's Jasmine, the Sultan's daughter," said the man.

"She is the girl I will marry," declared Aladdin.

The stall holder roared with laughter and said, "You don't understand. Her father will only allow her to marry a prince."

Aladdin spent the rest of the day thinking about Jasmine. When night fell, he got down the old oil lamp and rubbed it. With a flash, the Genie uncurled himself from the spout and hovered over Aladdin.

"What is your wish, Master?"

"The Sultan's daughter, Jasmine . . ."

"Ha!" laughed the Genie, "I wondered how long it would be before collecting more jewels became boring!"

"Jasmine," went on Aladdin, "I would like to meet her."

"Certainly, Master. Go up on to the roof and wait."

Aladdin went up onto the flat roof of his house and looked up at the stars. He thought about Jasmine's eyes, until he heard a swishing noise like the wings of a huge bird.

He was amazed to see a carpet flying through the night sky, with Jasmine sitting on it. It floated just above the roof and Aladdin helped her down.

"I was walking in the palace garden," said Jasmine, "when the carpet whisked me off my feet and brought me here. It must be magic!"

"Not as magic as the light in your eyes," said Aladdin. "Will you marry me?"

"I am lonely," said the princess, "and I can see that life with you would be exciting, but my father, the Sultan, says that I may only marry a prince."

"But I am a prince," said Aladdin. "I have a palace outside the city that is even grander than your father's."

"I don't believe you," laughed the princess.

Aladdin sent her home on the carpet. "I will call for you soon," he said as he waved her off.

As soon as Jasmine was gone, Aladdin rubbed the old oil lamp and the Genie appeared.

"Build me a palace that is even grander than the Sultan's."

"With pink marble domes and fountains?" asked the Genie with a yawn.

"Oh yes! And peacocks on the ground, because their tail feathers are like huge, beautiful eyes."

So Aladdin and his mother went to live in the grand palace. As soon as they had moved in, Aladdin invited the Sultan and his daughter to visit.

"Why have we never met before?" asked the Sultan.

"Because I have been searching the world for the most beautiful girl to be my princess," said Aladdin, taking Jasmine's hand, "and now I have found her."

The Sultan was dazzled by Aladdin's wonderful palace and the feast that the Genie had prepared for them. This must be a very rich prince indeed!

When his daughter asked to be allowed to marry Aladdin, he readily agreed.

Aladdin and Jasmine were married and rode home to their own palace in an open carriage. When they rode through the market, people threw flowers into the carriage for luck.

The wicked magician, who had been abroad, was amazed to see Aladdin sitting in the carriage beside the princess.

"Ah," thought the magician, "I must pay the happy couple a visit." He gave a horrible laugh and went off into the crowd.

A few days later, Aladdin decided to take his mother for a drive in their fine new carriage, while Jasmine picked some flowers. She was putting them in a vase, when she heard a voice outside calling, "New lamps for old!"

Princess Jasmine looked out of the window and saw a man, wearing a long, foreign-looking cloak, with a tray of shiny new gold oil lamps.

"I could give him that dirty old oil lamp of Aladdin's," she said to herself. "I've always thought it was strange that he's kept it. It looks so out of place among our gold dishes. Aladdin will be so pleased when he comes home and finds that I've got a lovely shiny new one."

She rushed out to the man and gave him Aladdin's old lamp.

"Here is your lovely new lamp," said the lamp seller.

The princess took it, and went back inside the palace.

At once the lamp seller, who was the wicked magician in disguise, rubbed the lamp and the Genie appeared with a great flash of light.

"What is your wish, Master?"

"Take this palace, and the princess, to the other side of the world!" roared the magician.

When Aladdin came home, he found a huge hole in the ground where his palace had stood.

Where was his palace, and his beautiful wife?

"The Genie will get them back," he said to himself. Then, with a thud in his stomach like the slab slamming shut on the cave, he remembered that the lamp was inside the palace!

"I will find Jasmine again," he vowed. "I won't stop until I find her, even if she's on the other side of the world."

Aladdin set out to look for his princess, living on scraps of food and sleeping under the stars. His gold coat became tattered and his feet grew hard and blistered with walking.

At last, after many years, when he had almost crossed the whole world, Aladdin saw the pink marble domes of his palace, shining in the distance through the morning mist.

"At last!" he said. "Now I must find my way back into the palace, and into my princess's heart."

Aladdin crept to the back door and stole inside. Along one of the corridors he found a beautiful girl scrubbing the floor.

"Aladdin!" she whispered. "You have come at last!"

He looked more closely, and saw that it was Jasmine, dressed in rags, but still with the same huge violet eyes.

"The magician is living in our palace," she sobbed, "and he keeps me as his slave."

"Where is the old oil lamp?" whispered Aladdin.

"He keeps it beside him at all times," said Jasmine.

"Does he ever have a nap?" asked Aladdin.

"Every night, after dinner, in front of the fire," said Jasmine.

"Then let's wait till then," said Aladdin. "We have waited so long, a few more hours won't hurt."

So Jasmine cooked an extra large dinner, and soon the magician was snoring gently in his chair. Aladdin tiptoed into the room and Jasmine pointed to the lamp, which lay on the floor beside the magician.

Aladdin took the lamp and rubbed it. There was a huge flash and the Genie appeared and hung just below the ceiling.

Jasmine jumped, and clung on to Aladdin. The magician woke up and tried to grab the lamp, but the Genie pointed a finger at him, and he stayed rooted to his chair, trembling with anger and fear.

"Master," boomed the Genie, rolling his eyes down at Aladdin.
"What is your wish?"

"Fly my princess and me, and our palace, back home to
China," said Aladdin.

They felt the ground beneath them lift, as if a tree was being
torn up by the roots.

The pink palace flew through the air and landed with a soft
thud back in China.

"Now what shall we do with the wicked magician?" asked Aladdin.

"Have you any ideas?" he asked the Genie, who was just about to get back into the lamp.

"The worst thing that I can think of," said the huge Genie, and his voice was quiet for once, "is to be shut up in that old oil lamp for a hundred years, until someone finds it and rubs it."

To Aladdin's horror, tears rolled down his fat cheeks.

"I hadn't thought of that," said Aladdin.

The magician was trembling with fear, and pressing himself against the palace wall.

"You wouldn't d-do it," he stammered. "Just think – you would have no more wishes!"

"I don't need a Genie to grant wishes now that I have found Jasmine again," said Aladdin. "I have everything I want."

Aladdin turned to the Genie.

"I wish that you would put the magician in the oil lamp and bury it back in the cave, where it can stay for another hundred years."

The Genie pointed a finger at the magician, who began a loud wail which grew fainter and fainter as he shrank smaller and smaller and disappeared down the spout of the lamp.

The lamp went hurtling out of the window, on its way to the cave in the hillside.

The Genie was sobbing quietly. "Free at last!" he gulped. "The magician has taken my place. How can I ever thank you?"

"Wish us luck," said Aladdin. "We will never be able to thank you enough."

"Before you go," he added, "I do have one last wish."

The Genie looked worried, because his magic powers had gone with the lamp.

"I'm afraid I can't produce any more riches or banquets," he sighed. "Not even one gold coin! Not even one giant shrimp!"

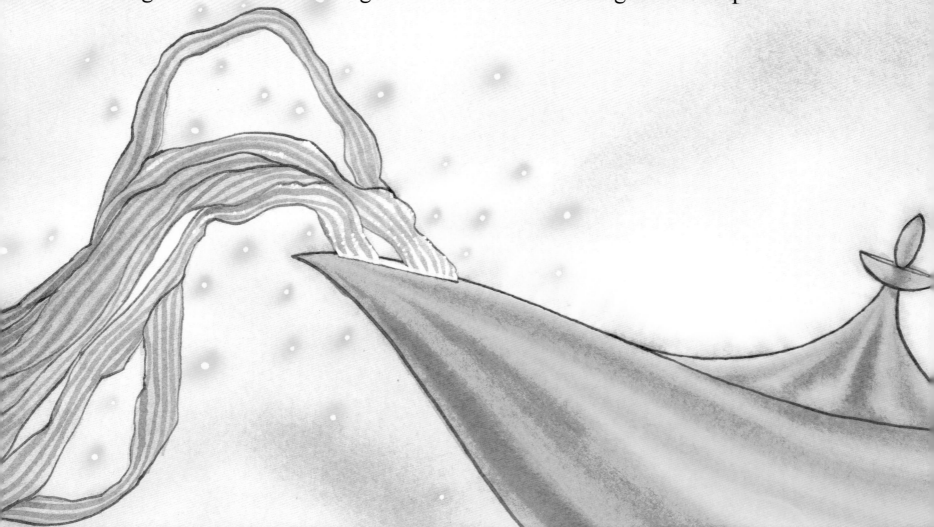

"My wish," said Aladdin, "is that Jasmine and I will live happily ever after."

A huge grin spread over the Genie's face.

"Your wish is granted," he beamed.

"I am sure you will live happily ever after."

And they did!